This book belongs to:

_____

_____

_____

First published 1999 by Walker Books Ltd
87 Vauxhall Walk, London SE11 5HJ

This edition published 2011

2 4 6 8 10 9 7 5 3 1

© 1999 Lucy Cousins
Lucy Cousins font © 1999 Lucy Cousins

"Maisy" Audio Visual Series produced by King Rollo Films for
Universal Pictures International Visual Programming

Maisy™. Maisy is a registered trademark of Walker Books Ltd, London.

The moral right of the author/illustrator has been asserted

Printed in China

British Library Cataloguing in Publication Data:
a catalogue record for this book is available from the British Library

ISBN 978-1-4063-3474-6

www.walker.co.uk
www.maisyfun.co.uk

Maisy's Bedtime

Lucy Cousins

WALKER BOOKS
AND SUBSIDIARIES

LONDON · BOSTON · SYDNEY · AUCKLAND

It's bedtime for Maisy and Panda.

Maisy closes her bedroom curtains.

Tuwoo, tuwoo, says the owl.

Maisy has a wash and brushes her teeth.

Maisy puts on her pyjamas.

She gets into
bed and reads
a bedtime story.

But where
is Panda?

Is he in the
toy box?

Oh, there he is!

Maisy switches off the light.

But she can't go to sleep.

Maisy needs
the loo!

So does Panda.

Maisy is really
sleepy now.

Good night, Maisy.
Good night, Panda.

Read and enjoy the Maisy story books

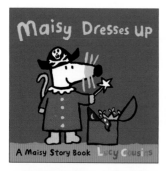

Maisy Dresses Up

A Maisy Story Book Lucy Cousins

Maisy's Bedtime

A Maisy Story Book Lucy Cousins

Maisy's Pool

A Maisy Story Book Lucy Cousins

Maisy Makes Lemonade

A Maisy Story Book Lucy Cousins

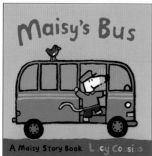

Maisy's Bus

A Maisy Story Book Lucy Cousins

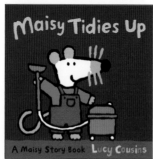

Maisy Tidies Up

A Maisy Story Book Lucy Cousins

Maisy Makes Gingerbread

A Maisy Story Book Lucy Cousins

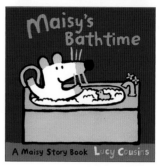

Maisy's Bathtime

A Maisy Story Book Lucy Cousins

My friend Maisy

Doctor Maisy

A Maisy Story Book Lucy Cousins

Maisy Goes Shopping

A Maisy Story Book Lucy Cousins

Available from all good booksellers

It's more fun with Maisy!

This book belongs to

....

www.makebelieveideas.com

Written by Hayley Down.
Illustrated by Clare Fennell.

"What's a Christmas?"

Hayley Down · Clare Fennell

make
believe
ideas

As the sun set on Christmas Eve, a sound BOOMED across the South Pole.

CRASH!

Four little penguins walked along

and tumbled

into a giant

hole!

There, inside that snowy pit, was a funny-shaped, snowy mound with two stripy legs sticking out and flippers that made a sound.

"What a weird bird,"
said Penguin Peg.

"That's no bird!"
said Penguin Paul.

"Give it a poke!"
said Penguin Pru.

Penguin Pete
said nothing at all.

Then something small burst out and cried,
"I'm no bird. I'm Ed the ELF!
I fell out of Santa's Christmas sleigh –
now I've crashed and hurt myself!"

The penguins felt bad for little Ed,
but they were also a bit confused.
They asked:

"What's an elf?"

"What's a sleigh?"

"What's a Santa?"

"What's a Christmas? And are you bruised?"

"Oh, bloomin' baubles!" shouted Ed.

"You've never heard of Christmas Day?

I'll teach you how to celebrate

'til Santa returns in his sleigh!"

"First, some sparkle is what we need
to bring some holiday glee."

"Let's try to find some twinkly treats
we can hang on a Christmas tree."

But in the snow, it's hard to find
decorations to gleam and shine,

so what the penguins used instead

were fish

and some boring,

old twine!

Ed said, "Next, we'll get kind gifts
to show our friends that we care."

"But remember, they should be thoughtful,
not just fancy, sparkly or rare."

The gift they found for their mother
was cute, but it wasn't quite right;
it was much too wet,
much, MUCH too big
and it gave her a little
fright!

Next, the penguins tried a carol
and though Ed sang with a smile,

the penguins' horrid, screeching squawks could be heard for miles and miles!

"We've done it **wrong**!" said Penguin Pete.

"We've **ruined** Christmas!" cried out Paul.

Ed said, "I don't know what you **mean**

because I'm having a **ball**!"

"This Christmas may not be fancy,

but the spirit we have is right.

Let's laugh and sing and just be glad

we're together this Christmas night!"

But then, Ed's golden pocket watch
struck twelve with a jingly chime.
"Oh, no!
The sleigh is almost here
and I haven't made a sign!"

His penguin pals knew what to do;
they had thought of the perfect gift!
They called all their friends and family
to make a sign in the snowdrift . . .

Santa flew over in his sleigh and from way up high, he could see some writing in the snow that said . . .

As Santa landed with a THUD,

he cried out, "Well, what a sight!

I'll spend the rest of Christmas here —

it's the perfect end to my night!"

They celebrated together,

then when it was time to say goodbye,

Ed promised that next Christmas . . .

he would be sure to drop by!

The end

Just Right for Christmas

For Adrian
B.B.

To my niece Gracie, with love
R.B.

First published in 2011 by Nosy Crow Ltd
The Crow's Nest, 10a Lant Street
London SE1 1QR
www.nosycrow.com

This edition first published in 2012

ISBN 978 0 85763 136 7

Nosy Crow and associated logos are trademarks
and/or registered trademarks of Nosy Crow Ltd.

Text copyright © Birdie Black 2011
Illustrations copyright © Rosalind Beardshaw 2011

The right of Birdie Black to be identified as the author
and Rosalind Beardshaw as the illustrator of this work has been asserted.

A CIP catalogue record for this book is available from the British Library.

Printed in Singapore

10 9 8 7 6 5 4 3 2 1

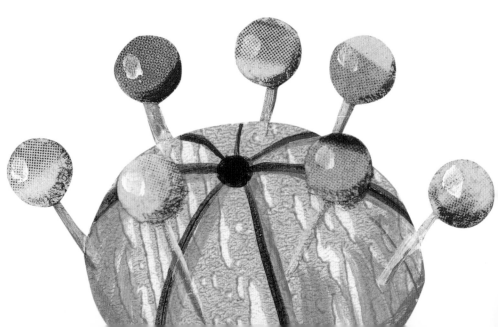

Just Right for Christmas

Birdie Black

Illustrated by

Rosalind Beardshaw

nosy crow

It was Christmas Eve, and snow was falling as the king strolled around the market. What should he see but a huge roll of beautiful bright red cloth!

"Oooh!" he said. "That cloth is so red and soft and Christmassy! It would be just right for a grand cloak for the princess!" And so he bought it and took it back to his castle.

In the castle, the king's sewing maids snipped and they sewed and they snipped and they sewed and, by lunchtime, they had made a beautiful long cloak for the princess. The king was delighted.

He wrapped it up in golden paper and silver ribbon.
"What shall we do with the scraps?"
one of the sewing maids asked.
"Oh, just bundle them up and put them outside
the back door," said the king.

Jenny, the castle kitchen maid, had finished work for
the day. What should she see on her way home but
a big bundle of beautiful bright red scraps?
"Oooh!" she said. "That cloth is so red and soft
and Christmassy! It would be just right
to make a jacket for my ma!"

When Jenny got home,
she snipped and she sewed and
she snipped and she sewed and . . .

. . . by tea-time, she'd made
a smart red jacket
for her ma.

She was very happy, and she wrapped it up in red paper with a green ribbon.

Then she bundled up the little scraps and put them outside the back door so her ma wouldn't see them.

Bertie Badger trotted past Jenny's house.
What should he see but a little bundle of beautiful
bright red scraps?
"Oooh!" he said. "That cloth is so red and soft and
Christmassy! It would be just right to make a hat for my pa!"

When Bertie got home,
he snipped and
he sewed . . .

and he snipped
and he sewed and . . .

by the time the clock
was striking six . . .

Then he bundled up the tiny scraps and put them outside the back door.

He smiled as he wrapped it up in some brown paper and tied it with string.

. . . he'd made a smart red hat for his pa.

Samuel Squirrel bounded past
Bertie's house. Suddenly, he stopped.
What should he see but a tiny bundle of
beautiful bright red scraps.
"Oooh!" he said. "That cloth is so red and
soft and Christmassy! It would be just right
to make a pair of gloves for my wife!"

When Samuel got home, he snipped and
he sewed and he snipped and
he sewed and . . .

by the time the moon was
rising, he'd made a beautiful
pair of gloves for his wife.

He wrapped them in a leaf
and tied up the parcel with a
piece of dried grass.

"It's just as well I've made her something
to keep her hands warm," he said.
"This winter wind is so chilly!"
A gust picked up the tiny scrap of red cloth that
was left over and blew it out of his window,
where it fluttered to the snowy ground.

It was nearly midnight when Milly Mouse
plodded past Samuel's house.
She was tired and cold, and the snow was falling on her
ears and whiskers. She had been looking for a nut to give
to little Billy for Christmas, but she couldn't find one.

As she passed the bottom of Samuel's tree,
she saw something red sticking out of the snow.

What could it be?

It was the tiny scrap of cloth!
"Oooh!" she said. "That cloth is so soft and
red and Christmassy. It would be just right
to make a scarf for my Billy!"

Billy was asleep when Milly got
home. She snipped
and she sewed and . . .

she snipped and she sewed
and, by the time the candle had
burnt down low, she'd made a
cosy scarf for Billy.

She didn't have anything to wrap it in, but she folded it carefully
and put it under her tiny sprig of Christmas tree.

And on Christmas morning,
the princess opened her
huge gold present.

And Jenny's ma opened her
big red present.

And Bertie's pa opened his small brown-paper present.

And Samuel's wife unwrapped her leaf.

And Milly gave little Billy his scarf.

Each present was so soft and red and Christmassy, and felt just right . . .

. . . just how Christmas should feel.